THE MYSTERY
AT
Death Valley

3

Published by Gallopade International/Carole Marsh Books. Printed in the United States of America.

Editor: Janice Baker
Cover Design: Vicki DeJoy
Content Design: Randolyn Friedlander

Gallopade International is introducing SAT words that kids need to know in each new book that we publish. The SAT words are bold in the story. Look for this special logo beside each word in the glossary. Happy Learning!

Gallopade is proud to be a member and supporter of these educational organizations and associations:

American Booksellers Association
American Library Association
International Reading Association
National Association for Gifted Children
The National School Supply and Equipment Association
The National Council for the Social Studies
Museum Store Association
Association of Partners for Public Lands
Association of Booksellers for Children
Association for the Study of African American Life and History
National Alliance of Black School Educators

Once upon a time...

Papa said …

Why don't you set the stories in real locations?

That's a great idea! And if I do that, I might as well choose real kids as characters in the stories! But which kids would I pick?

MIMI, PICK ME, PICK ME!

Christina

ME, TOO, MIMI, PICK ME, TOO!

Grant

Pick me!

You two really are characters, that's all I've got to say!

Yes you are! And, of course I choose you! But what should I write about?

National Parks!

SCARY PLACES!

Famous Places!

FUN PLACES!

Disney World!

New York City!

Dracula's Castle

GRAND CANYON

On the *Mystery Girl* airplane ...

I CAN FLY US anyWHERE!

Mystery Girl

Or aboard the *Mimi!*

Mimi

Take me to the Forbidden City!

Or by surfboard,
rickshaw,
motorbike,
camel ...

All great ideas!
I can put a lot of history,

MYSTERY,

legend, lore, and LAUGHS in
the books! We can use other boys and girls
in the books. It will be educational and fun!

Good stuff!

And so, Mimi, Papa, Christina, and Grant took off aboard the *Mystery Girl* and America's National Mystery Book Series—where the adventure is real and so are the characters! —was born.

START YOUR ADVENTURE TODAY!

READ THE BOOK!

GO ONLINE!

TRACK YOUR ADVENTURES!

APPLY TO BE A CHARACTER!

Table of Contents

BIG BANDAID BOO BOO

PAPA broke his ankle! So, he was unable to fly the Mystery Girl, and it was time for Mimi to research and write her new book, set in Death Valley in California.

"Phooey!" Grant complained. "If we don't get to go to Death Valley, Christina and I won't get to be in the book, will we?"

They were standing in Mimi's kitchen at "The Ranch," as Papa called their home in Peachtree City. Mimi was making lunch and they were about to carry their sandwiches and chips out to eat beside the pool.

"I don't know," Mimi said. "It's hard for me to imagine a mystery without you two characters in it!"

"But it's happened before, right Mimi?" asked Christina, already knowing the answer.

"Yes, of course," said Mimi. "Before you two were born, your mother and your Uncle Michael were the real kid characters in my books. Readers loved them just the way they love you!"

Grant was making peanut butter crackers, and a mess, all at the same time. "But they love us more, right, Mimi?" he asked, sure he knew the answer.

Mimi laughed. "Well, you'll have to ask them!"

"And soon we have to make room for cousins Avery, Ella, and Evan to be in the books, don't we Mimi?" asked Christina.

Mimi stacked food on paper plates. "As tall as you're getting Christina, you may outgrow being in the books. Maybe you could just write them for me?"

Christina giggled. She couldn't imagine that...or could she? She loved writing, but she liked designing houses more and thought she might want to be an architect when she grew up.

"Well as long as you don't kick the Great and Wonderful Grantster out of the mysteries!" Grant said. "You can't have a Carole Marsh Mystery without ME!"

"We'll see, Grant, we'll see," Mimi said absent-mindedly. She headed for the patio with an armload of crispy grilled cheese sandwiches.

"Oh, here, Great and Wonderful and Beautiful and Kind Mimi," Grant swooned, opening the door for her. He gave a deep bow.

His grandmother laughed. "Don't be so silly, Grant," she said. "I see right through your act, you know. I'm sure you'll be a character as long as you live."

"That's a relief!" Grant said, spewing cracker crumbs into the sunshine.

"Grant!" squealed Christina. "You've been eating more crackers than you've been making!"

"You bet!" her little brother said, spewing more crumbs right into his sister's face.

"Grrrrrrrrrr!" Christina grumbled.

PATIO PONDERINGS

As they settled around the patio table to eat lunch, Papa hobbled out on his crutches. "I smell peanut butter," he said.

Christina hopped up to pull a chair out for him. "I think Grant's even got peanut butter in his ears," she told her grandfather, who said, "Well, I think I'd rather eat PB on crackers. Thanks, anyway."

Mimi and the kids laughed. Papa was a big teaser, but he was bummed-out because of his leg, and in pain, and on medication, so he had been sleeping a lot.

"What's up?" he asked as Mimi passed the sandwiches.

"Not much since we can't fly to Death Valley," Mimi said sadly. "I guess I'll have to skip writing this book."

Papa looked stunned. Mimi never abandoned an assignment. Besides, he remembered something that she must have forgotten. "Woman," he began (which always made Christina and Grant laugh), "don't you remember long ago the first time we went to Death Valley?"

"Of course I do," Mimi said.

"Then why don't you recall that you wrote a Death Valley mystery back then?" asked Papa.

At first, Mimi looked confused. Then suddenly it was clear that she did remember what Papa was referring to. She snapped her fingers and smiled. "That's right! I was so fascinated that I wrote in the car as we traveled along. I was especially flabbergasted over Death Valley Scotty and his castle in the desert." Papa nodded.

Christina and Grant got very excited. "A secret, forgotten mystery?" Christina said.

"Who's Scotty? Where's Death Valley? And what desert castle?" Grant asked breathlessly.

"Let's finish our picnic lunch," Mimi suggested, "and then I'll tell you about our long ago trip to Death Valley. Maybe I can even find that book around here someplace."

"Oh, please do!" both kids begged.

"We could read it without having to wait for you to write it!" Grant marveled.

"But we wouldn't be in it," Christina said sadly, still disappointed over the cancelled trip.

"But I'll bet you could solve the mystery?" Papa said.

Christina and Grant gave him an **incredulous** look.

"We're the stars of mystery solving, Papa!" Grant said. "You know that!"

Christina grinned. "Yes," she agreed. "I can't imagine how Mimi even wrote a book without us," she teased.

Mimi teased back. "I can eat my lunch really, really slowly, then take a looooong nap."

"Oh, no!" the kids squealed. "Eat fast and we'll even clean up," Christina promised.

"Speak for yourself, Sister," said Grant, but he ran for the trashcan and a dishcloth.

A new mystery, set in Death Valley—IF Mimi could find it. That would be Mystery Number One.

REWINDING THE TALE

After lunch, Mimi refreshed her iced tea with lemon and mint and settled down to tell the kids about an early Mimi and Papa adventure.

"Papa and I had been traveling around California one hot summer," Mimi began. "We couldn't decide where to go next, so I got out the map and looked and suggested Death Valley. This was before we had the Mystery Girl so we were driving and taking all back roads, not interstates. I thought Death Valley sounded like a perfect location for a mystery book, of course."

"What is Death Valley?" Grant asked. "It sounds, well, deadly."

"It is!" Mimi said. "Or can be. Death Valley is a long, sunken desert basin surrounded by high mountains. It includes a place called Badwater, which is the lowest spot in the Western hemisphere—228 feet below sea level!"

"How can that be?" asked Christina. "It seems like if it is a sort-of shallow bowl, it would fill up with water and be a lake." To demonstrate, she poured the rest of her water onto her empty paper plate.

"That's what you might think," Mimi agreed. "IF it rained in Death Valley, but it hardly ever does!"

"So you mean it only rains once a month or something like that?" Grant asked, tossing potato chip crumbs into Christina's paper plate lake.

"Uh," Mimi began, "it only rains maybe once a year." She tipped the paper plate up and all the water poured out.

"Yikes!" said Christina. "Why that would just leave a...a...desert?"

"Exactly!" said Mimi.

Grant was amazed. "How did Death Valley get its name?"

Mimi sipped her ice tea. "During Christmas week of 1849, more than a hundred, half-starved **emigrants** tried to find a shortcut to the gold fields during the California Gold Rush," she said. "They decided to try what some people called 'The Valley of Burning Silence.' It was an appropriate name, because many of the emigrants died."

"But how?" asked Grant, always a tender-heart and concerned about people.

"They got dehydrated from lack of water, starved from lack of food, maybe got lost or hurt," Mimi explained. "Death Valley is just not a welcoming environment, you could say."

"So what made you and Papa think it would be so exciting to visit there?" Christina asked.

Mimi laughed. "Oh, you know me and Papa—if it's a challenge, and historic, and has intriguing names and places, we just have to go! And so we did."

"Was it fun?" Grant asked doubtfully.

Mimi frowned. "Well, yes and no. It's really getting warm out here, so let's go inside and get cooled off and I'll tell you more."

D
IS FOR DEATH

Inside, Papa was sitting with his leg up on a chair reading a book.

"What are you reading, Papa?" Christina asked.

Her grandfather stretched and yawned. "Oh, I thought I'd read some books we bought at Death Valley. If I can't take Mimi there to do more research and I can't take you and Grant there to see it, I thought I could help like this."

"Don't feel bad, Papa," Grant pleaded. "It's not your fault you broke your ankle. We can go to Death Valley some other time, right?"

"You bet, pard'ner!" Papa said. "While Mimi cleans up from lunch, why don't I tell you kids some stuff about Death Valley. Then when Mimi reads you her story you will enjoy it even more."

"Ok!" Christina and Grant said together. They gathered around Papa, being careful of his leg and foot.

Mimi called from the kitchen, "I'm listening, too, so talk loud."

"I always talk loud," Papa grumbled and the kids giggled. He pulled out a book. "Just listen to these names: 'Furnace Creek,' 'Last Camp,' 'Burned Wagons Point,' 'Stovepipe Wells,' 'Devil's Golf Course.'"

"Sounds like a treacherous place to visit," Christina mumbled.

"Dangerous, too?" asked Grant.

Papa nodded. "It was in the past, and it can be today."

"You mean even if we could fly out there today on the Mystery Girl, we might get in trouble?" Christina asked.

"If we were not prepared," Papa said.

"How do you prepare for a valley called Death?" Grant asked. He was not sure he wanted to go on a mystery book trip like that.

Papa pulled an old scrapbook out from behind his chair cushion. He opened it and tugged out a piece of wrinkled paper. "Here's the list of supplies Mimi and I took into the park." He handed the paper to Grant who read:

"12 bottles of water
 1 box of food
 2 maps
 2 extra gallons of gas
 first aid kit
 2 blankets
 flashlights and batteries
 toilet paper."

"I don't understand why you need blankets in a hot desert," Christina said.

"It's scorching hot in the daytime," Papa explained, "but when the sun goes down, it can be freezing cold."

"But aren't you in your motel by then, safe and sound?" asked Grant.

"Not if your car overheats and breaks down!" said Papa. The kids just stared at him.

"So you might have to spend the night in the car?" said Christina.

"And go outside to the bathroom?!" added Grant. "Where there might be coyotes and snakes and lizards and scorpions, not to mention sharp cactus spines to stick you in the backside?!"

Papa nodded.

"Who were the brave kids Mimi put in that mystery book?" Christina asked, sort of glad that it hadn't been her and Grant.

"Your Aunt Erin," Papa said. "She was your age back then."

Grant looked very serious. "And did she live to tell the tale?" he asked.

Christina started to giggle, then realized Papa was not smiling. In fact, he was frowning and looked very sad.

BROWNIE UP

Mimi came into the den with a plate of warm, chocolate-frosted brownies. "I thought you adventurers might need some energy," she said. "But what's with all the serious faces? Do you feel bad, Papa?"

The kids turned to hear his answer, but all they heard was a big "ZZZZZZHHH." Papa had fallen asleep, the scrapbook tucked under his arm.

"Shhhhh," warned Mimi. "I guess Papa's medicine made him sleepy. Let's go in the other room and eat our brownies."

"And you will tell us what happened to Aunt Erin?" Christina said.

Mimi frowned. "I will tell you more about our trip to Death Valley," she promised and led the way to the screened porch where there were more brownies and a pitcher of lemonade.

Christina and Grant settled down in big, cushioned chairs with their dessert.

"We're ready!" Christina said.

Mimi sighed. "Ok," she said. "Let's see how good my memory is. On a hot summer's day like this I feel like my brain is fried." She rubbed her hand through her blond curls.

"Mimi, please don't talk about fried brains while we are eating brownies, ok?" Grant asked.

Mimi nodded and picked up the thread of Papa's Death Valley story:

"You know Papa and I like to travel off-season a lot, but it didn't make any difference in Death Valley—it was still hot. Not so much early in the morning when we entered the National Park, but as the day went on. Right away, we were fascinated by the desert terrain. It was so different from our forestland here in Georgia. Also, the park is enormous, so it seemed like it could have been a hundred years ago, it was so desolate, and I felt we were alone in this gosh-forsaken place, except maybe for ghosts from that past."

"Ghosts?" Grant asked. "Real ones?" He shivered.

"I don't know about real ones," Mimi said, "but a lot of people have died in this place, so it just felt kind of creepy to me."

"Tell us!" Christina begged, reaching for a second brownie. For some reason, hearing about scary things made her hungry. Maybe it was just nerves. Or maybe the brownies were just really, really yummy.

Mimi sat back in her chair with that "I'm remembering" day-dreamy look. "I have an idea—let me tell you about a family who almost died. It was Christmas Eve in 1849. A woman named Juliet Brier and her sons, Columbus, John, and Kirk trudged across a dry creek bed crossing Death Valley. The walking was hard through the deep sand, and they kept sinking down up to their shoe tops."

"How old were the boys?" Grant asked.

"They were nine, six, and three years old," Mimi said. "They had come to the area with their mother and father, who was a minister. They were with a group called the 'Sand Walking Company,' which was trying to find their way through the desert to get to the gold fields.

"The group began their journey with lots of provisions," Mimi continued, "including a herd of cattle and wagons full of supplies. But they made a big mistake by taking a shortcut to get around some mountains. They ended up in Death Valley, one of the most barren places on Earth!"

"Gee," said Christina. "That must have been scary."

"It was," said Mimi, "and dangerous. Now, back to Juliet and the boys. The father went ahead to look for a campsite. Juliet and the kids stumbled on until they finally found him waiting for them around a fire ring. They thought that was the place they would camp, but he said not...that they had six more miles to trek!"

"Did they make it?" Christina and Grant begged together.

"They made it, finally, to the campsite, where they found a welcoming fire and a flowing spring," Mimi said. "It was Christmas day by then, only no one was celebrating. By that time, there was so little food left that they had to kill one of their oxen for Christmas dinner. At that meal, the group had a big discussion. It was decided that Mrs. Brier and the boys should stay at camp while the rest of the men pressed on toward California, where they would send help back to them."

"What did Mrs. Brier say to that?" Christina asked.

Mimi laughed. "She said, 'Absolutely not!' She had no idea how far the men had to travel or when they might be back. She feared that she and her boys would be lonely and scared, and might even die of thirst or hunger."

"So what happened?" Grant asked eagerly. It seemed like such a strange and frightening way to spend Christmas. He could not imagine it.

"When Mrs. Brier refused, they all pressed on. They had 150 miles of flat, hot, salty land to traverse. They left their wagons at Furnace Creek and only took what they could carry on their backs and on the few oxen left. After a couple of days, they met up with another group. It was two months before they finally got to safety. And even though the Brier family had lost all its possessions, Juliet Brier's decision had probably saved all their lives."

For a moment the children were silent, then Christina said, "So this was a story repeated many times in Death Valley over the years?"

Mimi nodded. "Maybe it was miners, or emigrants, or most anyone else, but when any of them entered Death Valley, it was truly using their smarts and luck that got them out alive—or not."

"Mimi?" Christina said somberly.

"Yes, Christina?" Mimi replied.

"Maybe you'd better read us the mystery book you wrote back then?"

Mimi nodded and picked it up...

THE MYSTERY AT Death Valley

A Word from the Author

In the late winter of 1992, I visited Death Valley. I came in "the back door" from Trona, and the landscape was already so desolate, I could not imagine how it could get worse enough to be called "death," but it could.

All the signs and warnings about heat and height and rattlesnakes and flash floods and getting lost and devil's-this and devil's-that was enough to make me want to turn around and go back to the Holiday Inn I had come from.

But what I found in Death Valley was life! An oasis of life: living history; colorful wildflowers; kids scooting on sleds through fresh snow on mountaintops . . . and splashing in hot springs on the valley floor below. Even the sand dunes were alive, moving invisibly on their way to nowhere.

The sky was certainly alive, alternately with full moon and stars, then with thunderhead, lightning and rain. At special times of the day, the rock walls were alive with colors as vibrant as a crazy quilt. The earth itself was certainly alive, still moving and groaning and growing, arranging and rearranging to suit itself as if trying to get comfortable, a seemingly impossible task.

The park was full of international life. Folks from all around the world shared discoveries and vistas and comments as they explored the monument and learned "ooh" and "aah" come in all languages. The wildlife— lizards and snakes and birds—seemed to welcome us to their unique world.

But two things most stuck in my mind: the speechless panorama called Dante's that made you feel out of this world . . . and a castle called Scotty's that reminds you that a few found Death Valley to be alive enough to call it home.

The character, Erin, is based on my niece Erin Kelly of Simpsonville, South Carolina.

I hope you enjoy your mysterious visit via this book to Death Valley and Scotty's Castle!

Carole Marsh

PROLOGUE:

THE DIE IS CAST

Erin was really ticked off. She guessed 9-year-olds weren't supposed to feel that way, but that was the way she felt anyway. Her parents had just lowered the boom on her: they were going to spend their summer vacation in DEATH VALLEY! Was it, she wondered, too late to enroll in summer school?

Go figure!: her dad liked the ocean; his secret ambition was to own a fish shop instead of being a hot-shot engineer. Her mom liked the water—ocean, lakes, creeks, streams, swimming pools, bathtubs, showers. And Erin, herself, wanted to be a marine biologist.

But, some weird somehow . . . some weird someway . . . the die was cast, and so instead of heading for someplace blue and green with cool breezes and alive with sea life (not to mention lots of other kids to hang out with), they were going to DEATH VALLEY.

"I think I'd rather die!" Erin said to her reflection in the dresser mirror. There was no way for Erin to know, in her nice little cozy house far away from Death Valley, California, in the pleasant little country town of Simpsonville on the outskirts of Greenville, South Carolina—that saying that was going to be a big mistake.

1
DEATH VALLEY SCOTTY

The ghost of Death Valley Scotty hovered on the near side of the estate. It was almost high noon. The castle—known as Scotty's Castle, after him—shimmered like a mirage in the 100-degree heat rising off the desert floor.

The white stucco glistened blindingly in the sun. The red terra-cotta tiles of the roof glowed as if alive with fire. The backdrop of massive mountains and brilliant blue sky really set off the castle, Scotty thought. A ruffle of green trees, thriving happily in their challenging environment, flapped as though in greeting to him, in the rare, surprising breeze.

Scotty liked to watch the visitors. He liked to see them "ooh" and "aah" and crane their necks, sashay across the bridge that joined the main house to the guest building, and climb the crenelated tower that looked right out of an Arabian knights' fairytale.

He especially liked to watch them snap roll after roll of photographs. Memories, he thought, memories were why he couldn't quite leave, couldn't quite bear to finally and completely give up his castle. Scotty felt he had to stay nearby, perhaps needed to stay close, to keep watch by noonday sun and moon-glade night over the castle blessed, or cursed, with his name.

But now, years and years after he was buried atop Windy Hill, overlooking the castle, he guessed he was literally much more a part of the death in Death Valley than the vibrant life that still (well at least for awhile each day) filled his former home.

Perhaps it was time for him to "rest in peace." Perhaps. Perhaps not.

2

DEATH VALLEY OR BUST!

In the back seat of the car, Erin tossed and turned in a snarl of blanket. A strange eerie dream roamed through her dark-haired head. There was a vision of a monstrously-large thing that glowed from without and within as though infested with, and borne by, gigantic fireflies.

Wind moaned sadly as if it was the chant of a ghost. And yet, there was the lilting tinkle of happy talk and satisfied laughter in the background.   First the wind.   Then the laughter.   Then the wind, as though two opposing forces sought control of this massive, night-flickering illusion.

Erin's mind's eye looked into the giant golden eye of . . . of what? A light of lace, panes of gold? A boy, a man? with a sack, leading a beast, or led by a beast, spun through her brain. A skinny black cross loomed, then grew larger as though zoomed in upon with a telescopic lens.

In her fitful sleep, Erin gasped, and the cross shattered into a mosaic of black: big black shapeless heaps, slats of black flew by, a lava-flow of black seemed to suck her down . . . down . . . down, until:

Her dad hit a pothole—BUMP!

Erin popped up, instantly wide-awake. She threw off the blanket and discovered she was damp with sweat. "Are we there yet?" she mumbled, rubbing her eyes.

"There yet?" her parents said in unison.

"You saw the map, Erin," her mom reminded her. "We are still hundreds and hundreds of miles away."

Erin did remember, dismally. She pulled out her lavender flashlight and aimed it, beneath the blanket, at her map. Home. Death Valley. Home. Death Valley. Hundreds and hundreds of miles. Home. Death. Life. Death. Then, never remembering clicking the light off, Erin fell into a heap and slept once more.

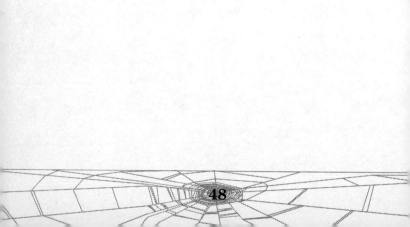

3
ROUTE 66

"Well, you seem to be in a little better spirits!" Erin's mom said.

"I'm in blueberry pancake spirits," Erin hinted. It was morning. It was Nevada. It was Route 66. And it was time for breakfast. "Daaaaaaaad," Erin pleaded when there was no response from the front seat. Her mother was busy reading *USA Today*; her father was singing *Achy Breaky Heart* at the top of his lungs.

They stopped for breakfast at a weird-looking diner that looked like something out of an old-timey movie.

"This looks like the kind of place we wouldn't normally stop at," Erin reminded her mother as they went through a door that was actually the heel of a big, blue boot.

"Oh, this isn't that kind of place," Erin's mother said, "this is nostalgic!"

Erin didn't know about nostalgic, but her nose told her the food smelled very, very good.

"Haven't you ever heard of Route 66?" her dad asked as they slid into a hot pink booth that had a gold star for a table. "It was the first real highway across the country, after the automobile was invented."

Erin gave her dad a dubious look. Her parents were old—thirty-something—but they weren't that old! And this wasn't exactly the interstate, she thought, looking out the window. This was nowhere—maybe even a few miles past it.

Her father passed lime green saguaro cactus menus around and continued his explanation. "It was a big deal to ride this road. The first motels were built along 66—nobody ever needed such a thing until they started traveling by car across America. Diners sprung up like daisies."

Erin looked around and decided that this place had probably been around as long as the first cars.

"They even made a TV show based on Route 66," her dad added before he stuck his nose in the menu. But Erin felt pretty sure he must be making that up. She decided on a short stack of "cactus cakes" with rattlesnake (orange) juice. Yum.

4

CACTUS PANCAKES & RATTLESNAKE JUICE

"Tell me about Scotty's Castle," Erin begged as they began their breakfast. If she was doomed to go there, she might as well get involved; and this desert castle was the only thing her parents had mentioned so far that really interested her.

Besides, she knew if she didn't ask, her parents would somehow instill enthusiasm and energy over a new adventure in her, whether she wanted them to or not. So, she might as well **instigate** the brainwash. Actually, what her mom told her was much more interesting than she expected.

"Well," her mother began, "it's the last kind of place you'd expect to see sitting in the middle of a desert. Scotty's Castle is a sprawling, two-story, Spanish villa at Grapevine Canyon on the north end of Death Valley. It's surrounded by desert and cottonwood and mesquite and cactus."

"Spanish villa?" interrupted Erin. "You mean that white stucco stuff with red tile roofs?" Houses built in that architectural style always looked romantic to her, and a little creepy, like they might be haunted.

"That's right," said Mother. "But picture lots of it: courtyards . . . towers with balconies . . . bridges from one building to another—and, secret passages."

"Secret passages?" Erin repeated.

Now Dad put in his two-cents-worth—he always did. "But the big secret is that this desert castle doesn't belong to the Scotty in its name at all!"

"It doesn't?" Erin asked, guzzling rattlesnake juice. "Then why do they call it

Scotty's Castle? How did this Scotty pull that off?"

"That's part of the castle's mysterious history and charming allure," said Mother, thrusting a booklet at Erin. "Read all about it!"

Erin knew that was coming. Her parents liked to get her interested in a subject that she swore she had no interest in. Then just as she was flooded with curiosity and questions, they hushed up and told her to "Read all about it." And, magically, they always seemed to have something to hand to her. Neat trick, hey? And one Erin had to admit, she always fell for— including this time. The castle sounded interesting, Erin also admitted . . . but it wasn't the beach.

5

WHO IS THIS SCOTTY?

As long as all they were doing was riding until the end of time, Erin figured she might as well read the biography of Death Valley Scotty her mom had given her.

There was a photograph on the cover of the booklet. It showed this Scotty character with his arms folded over a fat belly. He had a fat face too and wore a big, dumb-looking hat on his head. He didn't look like anyone she would like, Erin decided, but she'd been taught to not "judge a book by its cover."

Quickly she skimmed the boring parts:

- Born Walter E. Scott (hmm, that name sure seemed familiar) in Cynthiana, Kentucky, September 20, 1872 (boy, that was a long time ago, she realized).
- Spent his childhood on the road with his family who raced horses (that would be different, "but didn't he have to go to school?" Erin wondered).
- At age 11, headed out on his own to a Nevada ranch ("well, that's sure young to leave home," Erin thought, "especially to go to the wild, wild West!").

As Erin read on, she saw that there was more to this Scotty than first met the eye. As a young cowpoke, he worked with horses on ranches as far away as California. But Death Valley was the place that most appealed to him and he took a job at the Harmony Borax Works so he could live there. He was a swamper on the 20-mule teams that hauled the borax out of the desert.

But when he was just 16, he quit that job to join Buffalo Bill Cody's "Wild West Show" as a stunt rider! This started 12 years of touring. In a New York City candy store, he met his future wife. A short, hard stint in a gold mine came in handy later, after he was thrown out of the Wild West Show with no money and no idea of what he would do next to make a living.

But Walter E. Scott had a lot of talents—and an idea. An idea that would make him rich, famous, and perhaps, immortal! "Dad," Erin asked urgently, her dark eyes glistening, "When are we gonna get there?"

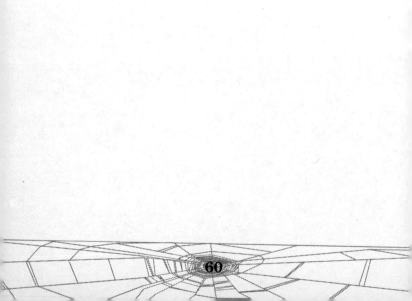

6

A GOLDEN IDEA

"Soon!" Dad said, and Erin knew that is all he would say until they actually pulled up in a parking space, if they had such things in a desert, so she settled back and read some more in the adventures of Walter E. Scott. It seemed that next he:

• Borrowed 2 gold specimens and talked a banker into grubstaking the mine in Death Valley that they had (not!) come from.

• Stayed in the public eye by pulling stunts to get attention, such as breaking the record time to travel by train from Los Angeles to Chicago, getting in a car wreck, being the star in a new play, getting shot and even disappearing in the desert for a month.

Suddenly everyone knew this amazing, fascinating character, now called "Death Valley Scotty," and while they might not always believe everything they read or heard about him, they all wanted to own part of his gold mine—the one that didn't exist!

One person was especially interested in Scotty and his mine. This was Albert M. Johnson, a wealthy insurance executive from Chicago.

Scotty and Mr. Johnson could not have been more different: Scotty was poor, Mr. Johnson was rich. Scotty was a stunt rider, Mr. Johnson was physically quite weak. Scotty lived the wild and wily life of a gold prospector, adventurer and media star, while Mr. Johnson sat in an office all day.

But they did meet, and the rest would be history!

In the meantime, just like a kid who has "cried wolf" once too often, Scotty got caught. The newspaper headlines said Scotty was a fake, that his mine was a phantom, and that he had even shot his ownself to get in the news. For awhile, Scotty's new name was "Mud"!

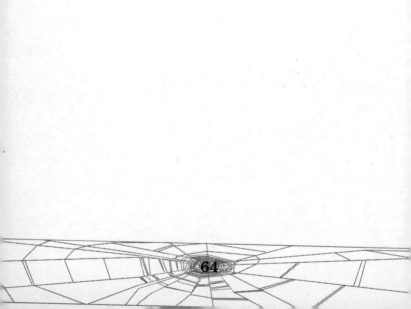

7

SCOTTY THE SKUNK

Boy, Erin thought, he sure had some nerve! But she couldn't help but feel a little sorry for someone as interesting as Scotty. Could things get worse for him? she wondered. And to find out, she read on, and indeed, they could!

Scotty couldn't put up and he couldn't shut up. Instead of growing up, he continued to act like a kid who'd gotten caught with his hand in the cookie jar. But finally, he went too far. He bragged that he had sold his mystery mine for $1 million and everyone began to sue him for all the money he owed them! At last Scotty had to admit, "My hole in Death Valley is all a myth." This should have been the end of Death Valley Scotty. Even his wife, with their new baby, was disgusted and left him. Scotty holed up in the desert, forgotten. Forgotten by everyone, that is, except Mr. Johnson!

Erin could hardly wait to turn the page and see what happened next. All this was true, but it surprised her that it was just as interesting as any made-up mystery she had ever read. But before she could flip the page, her dad said:

"You'll have to quit reading now."

"No!" said Erin. "Why?"

Her mother chuckled and plucked Erin and her book up off the backseat so she could see out the window. "Because we're here! We're in Death Valley."

This is not what I expected, Erin thought. The beach suddenly seemed far away . . . and

very boring. And what she saw out the car
window was incredible—absolutely incredible!

8

DEATH VALLEY

It was late afternoon. For all Erin knew they had traveled through a couple of time zones today when she hadn't been paying any attention. And while she hadn't been looking, they had entered another world, a world unlike any she had ever seen before.

Before her, spread Death Valley. She wondered how many earthquakes and volcanoes and quadrillions of years it had taken to produce the panorama before her.

For what she saw was an endless valley, burnt orange by the setting sun that was almost ready to fall behind a backdrop of the most gigantic bright red mountains she had ever seen.

Suddenly Erin understood why this place was famous, and why people came from all around the world to see it. And, as she read a sign by the side of the road,

DEATH VALLEY:
20 miles from water
20 miles from wood
40 feet from Hell

she also realized why it was so very scary and so very dangerous and so very exciting and so very . . .

"Well, don't you have anything to say?" asked her mother.

"I don't think we've ever seen you speechless," added Dad. "What do you think of this place?"

Erin had meant to say it loudly, but instead a hot, breathless squeak came out of her mouth. "Wow," she said. "Wow, wow, double, triple wow."

Then the sun plunked behind the mountains and darkness and a chill seemed to crawl across the desert floor and spew down the mountainside toward them.

"Let's get to our room," Dad suggested, and they all scurried into the car as though a rattlesnake had suddenly shaken its tail at them.

"Where are we staying?" Erin asked.

"A place called 'Furnace Creek,'" said Dad, and Erin gasped.

9
FURNACE CREEK

While her parents checked in, Erin roamed around the lobby. The brochures on the tables and the items posted on the bulletin board seemed to have one thing in common: DANGER! Erin decided she was going to like Death Valley a lot, maybe.

STAY ON PAVED ROADS!

BEWARE OF FLASH FLOODS!!

WATCH FOR RATTLESNAKES!!!

DRINK PLENTY OF WATER!!!!

IF YOUR CAR BREAKS DOWN, DO NOT LEAVE IT!!!!!

WATCH FOR ABANDONED MINES!!!!!!

There was even a "cartoon" of a family of people driving into Death Valley . . . and a carfull of skeletons driving out! "Funny," Erin said. "Real funny."

But the place they were staying was neat; it was like a rustic ranch but it had all the important modern stuff like air conditioning and bathrooms. As soon as they had a quick dinner, Erin rushed back to the room and plopped on the bed to pick up the adventures of Death Valley Scotty. She wanted to get to the castle part before they went to see it the next morning.

Erin could hardly wait.

10

DREAMING OF CASTLES

Sprawled across the bed, with the air conditioning humming, Erin tried not to think about the dark desert outside. Instead, she read in her book about the growing friendship between two men . . . and a growing castle, which for some reason was called "Scotty's":

• Mr. Johnson found his frail health improving greatly in the dry desert. He also enjoyed the jovial company of the now outcast Scotty. He began to buy land in Grapevine

Canyon. Mrs. Johnson also enjoyed coming to the Valley. But when she became fed-up with the tents and a shack they had to stay in ("sounds like Mom for sure," Erin said), she insisted her husband build a "real house."

• And, so he did. At first, it was just a set of three buildings, one of which included an apartment for their friend Scotty. Even though the buildings were plain, they had some pretty fancy stuff for the desert in 1922: a generator, refrigeration, and indoor plumbing!

• When people heard what was going on in the desert, they couldn't believe it. They were sure that character Death Valley Scotty was behind it. After all, can you imagine how much it must cost to get building materials and workers to the desert? Had he, they wondered, really found a gold mine after all? How else could he afford to build a castle in the desert?

• And though no one could explain it then . . . and no one can explain it now, the castle that was built became "Scotty's Castle." Mr. Johnson surely paid for it, and Mrs. Johnson had her say about how it would be built. But to everyone then, as to everyone now, it was still "Scotty's Castle"!

• And this wasn't any ordinary house in the desert. This was a real castle, complete with underground tunnels, three-foot thick fortress-like walls, possible secret passages, and more!

11

DAY 1: DAD'S DAY

As so often happens when you're the "kid" and everyone else is the "grown-up," Erin's plans were foiled. She guessed Dad never really had said they'd visit Scotty's Castle the very first day. But Erin was really disappointed when she learned at breakfast that her dad had the whole day planned for them—and the north end of Death Valley was not even on the list.

Her dad was so excited, "like a little kid," Erin thought. He even had on shorts and knee-socks, of all things, and red suspenders! And a straw hat!! Her dad never wore a hat. In fact, she mostly saw him in his business suit unless he was doing yard work in his dopey Bermuda shorts or headed for the golf course looking like a preppie in his polo shirt, khaki pants, and loafers.

"Oh, Dad, reaaaaaaly!" is all Erin ever said.

She was disappointed, but she didn't want to disappoint him by begging to change plans. Like the good kid she was, she sighed and shrugged and nodded agreeably at the castle-less **itinerary**.

Maybe she should be like the young Scotty and just run off and do her own thing. But as soon as this enticing thought crossed her mind, Erin pictured all the warning signs on the bulletin board, and one word—rattlesnakes—was enough to stop her. "When do we leave?" she asked begrudgingly.

"Right now!" said her father and he jumped up from the table and headed across the restaurant.

Erin saw that he had on Clemson University socks with big orange tiger paws on the side, and, that his blue boxer shorts were drooping down out from under the edge of his khakis. "Oh, Dad," she said. "Reallllllly!"

Her mother just shrugged her shoulders and grinned and plopped her own straw hat on her head and followed him. And reluctantly, so did Erin.

12

THE DEVIL'S CORNFIELD

They had packed enough thermoses and canteens of water (for themselves and the car radiator) to irrigate the desert, Erin thought, but she was secretly glad they had. Her mom had smothered her in SPF 30 sunscreen and insisted they wear long-sleeved shirts. "I'll bet Scotty wouldn't put up with this," Erin grumbled to herself. And this is what they saw:

• Mosaic Canyon: the walls of pebbles formed a colorful kaleidoscope; limestone rang like a bell when struck.

• The Sand Dunes: a park ranger told them this was a popular place for Hollywood movies to be made!

• The Devil's Cornfield: clumps of arrowweed that looked like corn; the plant's straight stems were used for arrow shafts by the Indians.

• The Ghost Town of Rhyolite: a gold-strike boomtown, which died out, but the ghosts of a railway depot, hotels, stores, and banks, plus a house made of 52,000 bottles! still baked in the sun.

• Badwater: the lowest spot in North America, 282 feet below sea level. They also saw Salt Pools, Natural Bridge, Artists Drive, Golden Canyon, and the Old Harmony Borax Works, where Scotty had once driven the 20-mule teams.

To Erin, the day was a hazy maze of colors, textures, patterns, sky, and heat, heat, and more heat. By the time they got back to Furnace Creek, just at dark, she was exhausted and went right to bed.

That night she dreamed of the names of the roads and passes they had bumped over: "Hell's Gate," "Bloody Gap"—but what really seemed to haunt her was Scotty and the word "ghost." She felt, or dreamed, he was calling her.

But she knew it was probably just the heat. Wasn't it?

13

MOTHER'S DAY OUT

The next morning, Erin had a headache.

"Drink more water today," Dad suggested.

"Eat more salt," said Mother.

What they didn't say was, "Let's go to the castle,"—and they didn't! It seemed her mom had her Death Valley shopping list today and Erin knew what that meant!

Indeed the day was just as she had expected. It was like Death Valley Mall, and

Mom was eager and determined to shop until Erin dropped. What they saw included:

- Zabriskie Point: eroded into beautiful, but weird, formations.

- Dante's View: at almost 7,000 feet above sea-level; Erin felt she could not get her breath, but maybe that was because the view was breath-taking!

- The Devil's Golf Course: "18 holes" of jagged rock salt spikes; "No hole-in-ones here!" said Dad.

- Skidoo: a ghost town, exactly 23 miles from Telescope Peak and water; where the phrase "23 Skidoo!" came from.

- Aguerreberry Point: a spectacular view up Emigrant Canyon—waaaaaaaaaaaaaay up Emigrant Canyon!

• Charcoal Kilns: huge bee-hive structures that at one time made charcoal for processing gold and silver.

• Mahogany Flats: at last they were in trees—junipers and mountain mahogany.

When they got back, once again just at dark, Dad was dead-on-his-feet. Erin once more collapsed into bed. But her mom had enough energy left over to start hitting the gift shops!

This night, Erin dreamed about Dante and Devils and blazing fires. It was almost morning before Scotty called to her again.

14

BAD TO THE BONE

"D, d, d, duh . . .," Erin sputtered the next morning; she thought she was still dreaming. Her mouth felt like it was stuffed with cotton.

Her eyes were stuffed with rock-size grit. Her muscles felt as if she had wrestled a passel of rattlers. Someone was calling her name: "Erin? Erin? ER-IN!"

"Scotty?" Erin said thickly, her eyes still closed.

"Mom!" Mom said. "Wake up! Talk to us."

Erin squeaked open one eyelid which felt as thick as her tongue. She was still in bed. Hovered over her were her parents and a strange face.

"Scotty?" she asked again.

"Give her some water," said Dad; he thought she was coughing.

The strange face laughed, and Erin opened her other eye. "Give her lots of water . . . and lots of rest," said the face. "She'll be just fine—it's just the Death Valley disease."

Disease! What was this stranger talking about? Suddenly Erin was wide awake and struggling to sit up. Her mom held her down. Erin fought back. She had seen that cartoon of the skeleton family!

"Calm down, kid," Dad said, thrusting the water at her again. "You just overdid it yesterday and had a little heat stroke. Gotta stay put today."

Stay put? Once more Erin struggled to sit up. She couldn't stay put! They were running out of days. They'd had Dad's Day and

Mom's Day, and now, today, was Erin's Day: the day to go to Scotty's Castle.

But it wasn't that day at all. In spite of her squirming and protests, Erin was forced to stay in bed and rest. It was probably a good thing because she slept most of the day, but she did have the strangest dream.

It was about Scotty, of course, but this seemed to be the real Scotty, not the overweight, aging man on the front of her book. This Scotty was young and slim and trim and handsome. He wore a brilliant white shirt and a blood-red tie, a white Stetson hat perched atop his head.

In Erin's dream, Scotty was holding a crisp white newspaper with the headline: DEATH VALLEY SCOTTY: AMERICA'S #1 MYSTERY MAN!

A crowd of people were gathered around Scotty; some squiggled as fast as they could with their pencils on notepads. His blue eyes seemed to twinkle as he spoke; he was propped against a car, his hat shoved back on his head. In her dream, Erin only caught snatches of what he said:

"It's got a 225-horsepower engine, and the square doo-hickey on the side is a trick cooler for Death Valley summer driving . . . she'll do 125 out in the desert as easy as pie!"

Then he seemed to be talking about the castle. "The gates alone cost $8,000 and there's $168,000 worth of iron in it!"

But every time Erin thought she was catching on to what he was talking about, he switched subjects. "Movies! I could easily be in them Westerns. I was a cowboy with Buffalo Bill for 12 years!

". . . millions in gold and silver coins . . ." Scotty was saying, and then he seemed to look past the crowd around him. His twinkling eyes seemed to look right into Erin's sleeping eyes. "Well, are you coming?" they seemed to say. "Or not? 23 skidoo, kiddo, 23 skidoo!"

When Erin finally woke up, it was night, and it was doing the strangest thing: it was raining!

"Sure, it rains in Death Valley," said Dr. Stone, who had come back by to check on Erin. "That's why they have those flash flood warnings everywhere. How do you think those alluvial fans got formed?" he asked.

Erin was sure she didn't know since she didn't know what an "alluvial fan" was in the first place.

Thunder popped and lightning whizzed through the sky, then it was silent.

So was Erin when her Dad said, "I'm glad you're feeling better. You know we're going on to Nevada tomorrow?"

No, Erin thought, she didn't know! So much for Scotty; so much for Scotty's Castle.

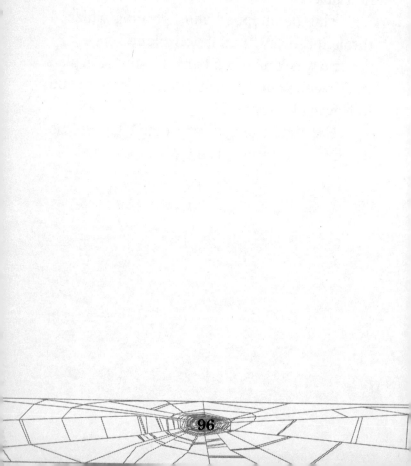

15

SAVED BY THE BELT

But they didn't leave the next day after all; they couldn't—Dad's car wouldn't run—something about the belts. So it went to the shop. And they went on one last tour.

"I'm glad to spend an extra day in the Valley," said Dr. Stone. "Let me take you folks to one of my favorite places at the monument." He didn't say where that favorite place was, but Erin had a feeling she knew!

Sure enough, they headed up the long road that had signs pointing to Scotty's Castle.

Dr. Stone knew a lot about the history and geology of the park and stopped along the way to point out different types of rock formations or blooming things with neat names like "rabbit bush," "turpentine broom," "bladderpod," "gravelghost," "globemallow," and "locoweed."

Erin learned what an "alluvial fan" was and that you pronounce words like "Gila" and "Hila," as if they started with an "H."

Everything was going wonderfully, until they reached a sign that said "Scotty's Castle This Way," and Dr. Stone made a turn down a road that went the opposite direction!

Erin didn't say anything; perhaps he was taking a back road. Maybe he just wanted to surprise them. And he did, all right. He surprised them by climbing to the top of a ridge to his favorite place: a big, giant hole in the ground!

"This is Ubehebe Crater," Dr. Stone explained. Mom and Dad were already out of the car with their cameras aimed at the void below.   In a daze of disappointment, Erin dutifully followed.

"It's 2,400 feet in diameter and was formed when a volcano erupted about 1,000 years ago," Dr. Stone added, waiting politely for their amazed response.

Erin realized that something Mother Nature built was supposed to be a lot more important and interesting than some dumb, old castle.

Wasn't it?

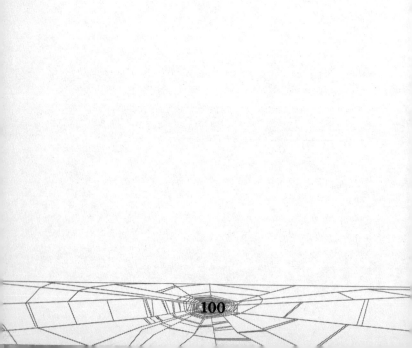

16

TRIPPED UP BY A CRATER

It seemed they stayed forever. Dad wanted to climb down into the monstrous crater and take pictures. Mom wanted to climb up to the highest peak over the crater for her snapshots.

Dr. Stone seemed to want to talk to everyone visiting the crater, especially if they were tourists from somewhere else in the world besides America. "Got to keep up my global connections," he said cheerily.

Then they had a picnic. The adults talked; Erin daydreamed; but as the sun faded in the sky, so did her dream. She didn't want to complain, but she could explain why she felt near tears, only no one wanted to listen. Besides, Erin wasn't a baby. She couldn't do everything she wanted to; she knew that. She was so deep in her thoughts that she did not hear Dr. Stone say to her parents, "Well, if we leave right now, we just have time to catch the last tour."

All Erin knew was that suddenly all these slow-poke adults were in a big rush to get to the car and head back. She followed.

That's why Erin was shocked when, a few miles later, she looked up and saw a mirage before her eyes. It was a gleaming white castle, Spanish in style, surrounded by rolling hills and towering peaks. The castle was capped by a tile roof as red as blood and nestled in strange-looking cactus plants of all kinds, many of them blooming in a variety of colors.

In her mirage, water splashed and tinkled. But her imagination was suddenly interrupted by her mother's irritated voice, "Erin? Erin! I thought this was what you wanted to see."

"What?" she said absent-mindedly.

"What?" her mother repeated in aggravation. "Scotty's Castle, that's what. Here's your ticket. Let's go; this is the last tour for the day. The others have already gone inside."

For the first time, Erin realized that the mirage had not vanished. She took the magical ticket and finally followed her mother toward the door.

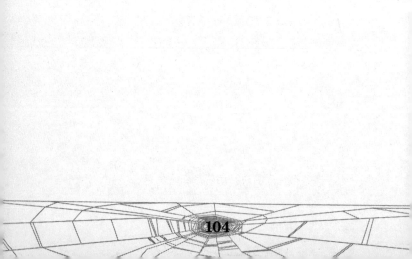

17

MIRAGES AND SHADOWS

Erin couldn't believe it! She was finally here at Scotty's Castle. She could hardly take her eyes from the edifice, which was worthy of the most wonderful of fairytales. The turret with its latticed windows especially appealed to her. She pictured Rapunzel letting her hair hang down and Romeo calling up to Juliet. But she didn't want to miss the tour, so she hurried on.

Still, no matter how quickly Erin moved through the courtyards and rooms, she never seemed to catch up with the others. This meant that she had her own private tour of Scotty's Castle. Since the afternoon was getting later and the sun was sinking behind the hills, the interior of the castle was very creepy.

It was surprisingly cool inside the building, almost chilly. Erin climbed a narrow path of curving steps up into the tower. She wondered if she had gone the wrong way.

Finally, she came into a room that surely was the Music Room. It was almost like a chapel. Dark wood arched over the ceiling and heavy tapestries covered the curved windows. All the furniture was large and dark and heavy. A Phantom-of-the-Opera chandelier hung down like a wrought-iron skeleton in the center of the room.

Are those real Tiffany lamps? she wondered. The twin kaleidoscopes of multi-colored glass shades spewed eerie colors around the room. Erin shivered.

Suddenly, the monstrous pipe organ in the room came to life with a burst of **ominous** tones. Erin jumped! She backed into a table and a glass vase tottered precariously. Hands shaking, she steadied it. "Right, Erin," she muttered, "break a priceless antique."

She tried to calm herself. The organ must be on a timer, she figured. But what about the shadow of a figure in a Stetson hat moving across the wall?!

18

THE GRANDE HALL

With a squeal, Erin jumped into a narrow hallway. She passed a maze of what must have been guest rooms, each also dark and clotted with thick rugs, tapestries, heavy furniture, and evil-looking wrought iron. All seemed to have Indian-style, kiva fireplaces.

It surprised her to see real bathrooms in the house. They weren't very modern, but they were colorful since the walls were plastered with all kinds of fancy Spanish tile in colors you could only call mustard or red mud.

She could have stopped to use one, frankly, but she was too scared.

It seemed to be getting darker all the time; but not so dark that she couldn't see the faces of statues and carvings and portraits staring at her in an accusing way.

At last Erin saw a glimmer of light and headed toward it. She discovered herself on a second-story bridge that ran between the buildings and over the courtyard. In spite of her rush, Erin stopped to look. It was quite a sight! She felt like she was standing on a terra-cotta capped jewel in the middle of a desert that seemed to spread out forever. Light and shadow played across the floor of Grapevine Canyon and the walls of the stucco castle. She could see why Scotty wanted to call this place his, whether it was or not.

Suddenly, she heard the sound of footsteps behind her and Erin scurried on. Determined to find her way back downstairs, Erin sped through the next hallways and rooms and down a flight of stairs where she found herself on a balcony overlooking what obviously was the living room or Grande Hall or whatever they called it.

It was a beautiful room, like something out of *King Arthur and the Knights of the Roundtable*. But since it was on the lower story, it got even less of the failing light than the upper rooms. Erin had to look hard to see which way was the way down. She spied a staircase and fled down it and into the large room. There! She could see the way out: a massive wooden door. But then she could also see that between her and escape was a long, chocolate-colored leather sofa. And on it sat a man in a hat.

19

GREETINGS FROM BUFFALO BILL

Erin gave out a little cry, and holding her fists tight beneath her chin, she gritted her teeth and ran for the front door. But as she passed the man, he reached out his hand and grabbed at her. He said something too, but Erin could not hear, for she had run into another room and slammed the door behind her!

It was a bedroom. There was a large bed with a headboard carved with a mountain lion, cactus, and a bighorn ram. In the corner, sat a desk with an uncomfortable-looking wooden chair in front of it.

Erin sat there, trying to catch her breath. She felt someone watching her, she knew she did. Finally she looked up and looking back at her was "Buffalo Bill" himself, or at least a large portrait of him hanging on the wall was. Suspicious, Erin looked around the dark room once more. And there on a hook hung a white Stetson hat and a blood-red necktie!

Suddenly, there was a great banging on the wooden door! And then from somewhere behind her, Erin could hear her name being called, softly, repeatedly. "Erin . . ."

It seemed to come from just outside the room. Erin was petrified, and she was trapped! Did she dare open the wooden door to the living room? Was there help or horror on the other side? But who in the world could be calling to her? Did she dare venture outside to see?

Dr. Stone had talked about rumors of secret passages in the house, including one in Death Valley Scotty's bedroom. Could she escape that way? Or was something else bad going to surprise her? She moved off the carpet beneath her feet, wary of what trapdoors might be hidden below.

At the edge of the carpet, Erin tripped. She grabbed at the wall. Her hand caught her fall because it had grasped an odd metal object. Erin twisted it and was surprised to see a hole of light about the size of a quarter. She peered into it . . . and a twinkling blue eye stared back at her. Erin screamed.

20

SEEING THINGS EYE TO EYE

"Erin, is that you?!" It was her mother's voice.

"Yyyes," Erin answered weakly. "Where are you?"

"I'm on the other side of the door, silly," her mom said. "Open it!"

Erin did as she was told, and when the door was open, she discovered her mother bent over looking into a hole in the wall. She looked up when Erin came outside. "Seems sneaky Scotty had a clever way to see who his visitors were before he answered the door," her mom explained.

"You mean that was your eyeball?" Erin asked.

Her mother laughed. "Well, who else's?"

"And you were calling me too?"

"Of course," answered her mother in exasperation. "We've been looking everywhere for you. Now go open that other door."

"What?" said Erin. "Are you sure?"

Her mother breezed past her. "Of course, I'm sure. The security guard is on the other side. He saw you go by and tried to catch you, but you wouldn't stop." She gave her daughter a critical look as she unhinged the latch on the door. "What's gotten into you, girl?"

Erin just stood there feeling ridiculous. She clasped her hands behind her back and hung her head. "Nothing," she said. "Nothing at all."

Her mother dismissed the guard, and then her father and Dr. Stone showed up. Erin was relieved that they didn't seem to be at all concerned that she had been missing. She knew her dad was used to her mom disappearing for hours on historic house tours and even in Walmart.

"Had a nice tour?" asked her dad.

"Sure Dad," Erin said. "But can we go now?" She had had her fill of Death Valley Scotty and his castle.

"Oh no!" said Dr. Stone. "We can't leave yet. We have to go up Windy Hill."

"What's up there?" Dad asked.

"Why, Scotty, of course!" answered Dr. Stone.

Erin groaned.

21

WINDY HILL

Even though it was all but dark, they climbed the steep hill behind the castle. The desert around them had taken on a sinister, threatening look of jagged mountain peaks and dark clouds. Erin was sweaty, but she also felt a chill. The rocks crunching beneath her feet was the only sound as they trudged upward.

Erin should have known what they'd find at the top, but she hadn't suspected. It was Scotty's grave. A cross and a bronze marker designated the spot where he and his dog,

Windy, had been buried. Dr. Stone aimed his flashlight at the marker and in the splash of light Erin read:

WALTER "DEATH VALLEY" SCOTT
(1872-1954)
"DON'T COMPLAIN. DON'T EXPLAIN."

"He was a real con artist, wasn't he?" Dad said.

"Oh, I don't know," said Dr. Stone. "He got what he wanted, but he also gave back—to the Johnsons then . . . and to visitors here today."

"Well, I don't know if he complained or not," said Mother, "but he sure never explained himself. What do you think, Erin?"

Erin was lost in her own thoughts. It was interesting listening to adults' opinions, but she had her own. And she didn't want to explain them either. "I think," she said, "we should go."

In silence they headed back down the rocky path, the castle twinkling in a golden glow against the dark desert backdrop. Halfway down, Dr. Stone pointed out into the desert. "You know, Scotty had his own private ranch a little ways from here. It was just a rustic three-room house with no electricity or running water, but it was his favorite place to be."

"More than the castle?" Erin asked.

"Oh, yes," said Dr. Stone. "A lot more than the castle."

"How mysterious!" said her mother.

But Erin thought she understood.

The adults went on ahead toward the parking lot. Erin lagged behind, hating to leave this corner of Death Valley that seemed so filled with life, even if the Johnsons and Scotty were dead. Of course, people called a desert dead too, when as Erin had learned, it was alive with life: plants and animals and changing earth and even, surprisingly, water.

Erin looked up. "What?" she called into the darkness.

Up ahead, her father spun around. "What what?" he called back to her. "We didn't say anything."

Erin nodded. Had it only been the wind or the gurgling water in the nearby creek? No, she thought, neither of those, and smiled to herself in the darkness. She knew she had heard her name . . . and she knew who had called it.

Quickly, she ran on to catch up with the others. It was time to go home.

22

GOODBYE TO SCOTTY

Never, in all her born days, would Erin have believed that she would hate to leave a place like Death Valley. She stood by the side of the road in the breaking dawn. Her dad was pumping gas; her mom was pumping coffee. Slowly, Erin did a 360-degree pirouette, taking in all the history . . . all the mystery . . . all the beauty . . . all the suspense of the place.

When she stopped, flat-footed on the already beginning to steam pavement, a sudden cool, almost chilly, waft of breeze tapped the back of her sweaty neck. She turned in the direction it had came from and found herself looking right down the road that led to Scotty's Castle. Erin smiled.

Just as suddenly, an enormous shadow loomed over Erin's back and spread far and wide onto the road before her. She muffled a shriek and spun around to see her dad standing right behind her, hands on his hips, a grimace on his face.

"I want you in the car, young lady," he said, "before you bake like a chocolate-chip cookie."

Erin shook her finger at him teasingly. "Don't complain! Don't explain!" she half warned, half pleaded.

Her dad grinned and hoisted her up on his shoulder, her legs dangling far down his back.

"Really, Dad," Erin groaned, "I'm getting a little big for this, don't you think?"

But her dad just kept striding toward the car, Erin bouncing like a ragdoll. "You certainly are," he agreed. "That's why I think I'd better do it every chance I get!"

Erin laughed. It was ok with her. "Hey, Dad, can we go to the Grand Canyon next year?"

"That mother-of-all-holes-in-the ground?" he responded. "I can just imagine you getting lost there!" He plopped Erin in the backseat of the car.

"Better get used to me going my own way, Dad."

"Never!" he insisted. "And I'll tell you why . . ."

Erin shoved her finger into his chest sharply, and he backed away.

"I know . . . I know!" he said. "Don't complain; don't explain."

Erin said not a word. She just nodded very knowingly at her father, then snuggled back into the car seat and began to daydream about the Grand Canyon!

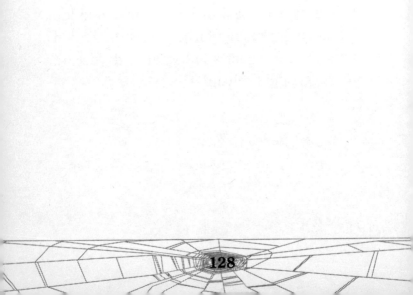

POSTLOGUE

THE MOST MYSTERIOUS MAN IN AMERICA

Scotty stood at the edge of Grapevine Canyon and took one last look at the castle . . . his castle. He guessed it was the little girl that had convinced him. After all, the castle seemed to be in good hands. People enjoyed the tours. But all of them, until this recent young visitor, had followed the designated path, not broken any rules.

He chuckled; it seemed a long time since he had laughed. But just picturing her tearing around the castle broke him up! Then hiding in his old room. And the look on her face when she saw that eyeball in the peephole!

"How refreshing," he thought, "to see a spirited youngster take a different path, follow the road less traveled." Why she'd gone through the house completely backwards—and just look how much more fun it had been! An adventure. Just like Scotty used to have, even when he was as young as she, which had been a long time ago now.

Maybe it wasn't too late, Scotty thought. He'd always been a restless spirit, even when he was alive. So why not go on an adventure himself? He shoved his white Stetson back on his head and tugged at his red tie. With a final glance at the castle—his castle—he turned in the sand and started down the long, lonesome road.

But where, he wondered, to go? Then a thought, like the twinkle of the star rising over the valley of Death, came to him. "How about the Grand Canyon?" Scotty moved on down

the road into the night.   His dog Windy,
keeping a sharp eye out for rattlers, followed.

THE END

NOW LEAVING DEATH VALLEY

"Mimi, that was a great story!" Christina said, when her grandmother finished reading.

"I just wish we'd been in it," Grant grumbled.

"It really makes me want to go there, in spite of the bad stuff," Christina said with a sigh. "Too bad Papa can't fly the Mystery Girl with his broken ankle."

"I know," said Mimi. "I would love for you two to see that desolate landscape, all the signs and warnings about heat and height and rattlesnakes and flash floods and getting lost!"

"Yeah," said Grant, "and I want to go to all those places named Devil's this and Devil's that. Especially the one named Devil's Food Cake!"

Christina and her grandmother laughed. "Grant, how can you be hungry for more chocolate? You just gobbled down half a dozen brownies," Mimi teased.

"Well, I want to see the oasis places you talked about," said Christina. "It seems so strange that you could find water and wildflowers, and even snow in the desert."

"I want to ride the moving sand dunes!" said Grant. "And see the big storms and a full moon over that crater and all the colored rocks and the lizards and snakes."

"If we ever get to go, I'm staying as far away from you as possible, Grant!" Christina said and cringed. "We are definitely interested in different things, that's for sure!"

"No one mentioned Scotty's Castle," Mimi reminded her grandchildren.

Christina and Grant looked surprised. "We thought you made that part up!" Christina said.

"Yeah," added Grant. "Who ever heard of a castle in a desert? I thought that was the fiction, not the faction, part of the mystery."

Mimi laughed. "Now you kids know if I put facts in a book that they are true, even if they are a bit flabbergasting."

Christina gave her grandmother a suspicious look. "Mimi, I still think you are pulling our leg. There wasn't really a castle, was there?"

Grant yanked his right leg as he scooted his bottom across the floor. "Yow!" he squealed. "The ghost of Death Valley Scotty is pulling my leg...he's pulling me across the floor...he's pulling me to the refrigerator...he's opening the door...he's looking for lemonade. Help! Help!"

Christina and Mimi burst out with laughter. Grant was always so silly, but always

*entertaining. They often thought he should grow
up and be an actor, or maybe a comedian.*

*"Grant, I will be glad to pour you some
lemonade," Mimi said. "All you have to do
is ask."*

*"It's not for me," Grant pouted. "It's for
Scotty. He says he's been thirsty a long time."*

Mimi poured them all some lemonade.

*Suddenly, Papa clumped-clumped-clumped
into the room on his crutches. "What's all the
ruckus in here? I was taking a nap and I
thought the house was falling down around
my ears."*

*As Mimi explained that she'd just read The
Mystery at Death Valley to the kids, Papa
snapped his fingers. "You know, I feel better after
my nap. I think if I had a brownie and some
lemonade, I could ride the Ladybug golf cart
over to Falcon Field and check on the Mystery
Girl. You never know when I might be able to
fly again."*

*Mimi smiled. She knew Papa was just
bored and that it would be quite awhile before he*

could fly. "That's a great idea, dear," she said,
and packed him a snack for the ride.

COME BACK
AGAIN SOON

After Papa left on the golf cart, Mimi and the kids headed out to the pool for a swim. As Christina and Grant lay on floats on the water, Mimi told them more about Scotty's Castle so that they would believe she was telling the truth.

"Look at this booklet," she said, holding it up like she was hosting a library, story-hour poolside. She flipped through the pages with pictures of Scotty's Castle.

"See," she said. "Here's a map. It shows Grapevine Canyon, the castle with its 25 rooms, and the 9 outbuildings. There's a garage and a bunkhouse, stables for the horses, a fresh water spring, a cook house, gas tank house, solar water heater, courtyard, power house, chimes tower, gravel separator, guest house, swimming pool..." Mimi rattled off.

"Guest house? Pool?" squealed Grant, splashing his way closer to see the page. "So if we went to Death Valley, could we stay at Scotty's Castle? It sounds cool!"

"Of course not," Christina chided her brother. "It's a historic site."

"Then I could greet all the visitors," Grant said. "Maybe they would think I was Death Valley Scotty!"

Christina splashed him. "Maybe they would think you were a pesky little brother, that's what they'd think." Grant splashed her back. Mimi closed the book and backed away to keep from getting wet.

Suddenly the little red Ladybug golf cart sped through the backyard gate and up to the pool. Papa was grinning.

"Pack your bags!" he said. "We're going to Death Valley!"

"HOW?" squealed Christina.

"HOW?" hollered Grant.

"HOW IN THE WORLD?" Mimi asked, looking at Papa's cast.

Papa grinned even bigger. "Old Joe, the mechanic, rigged up a special way for me to get *my foot, cast and all, in the Mystery Girl so I can fly her with ease!" He waved his cowboy hat in the air and said, "So let's round 'em up and head 'em out, 'lil doggies!"*

Before Papa could slap his hat back on his head, the kids jumped out of the pool and scampered into the house to get dressed.

Mimi just stared at Papa. "Are you sure about this?" she asked.

Papa gave her a big, fat kiss on her cheek. "I saw that!" Grant called from inside the house. "TOO MUCH MUSH!"

"Of course, I'm sure," said Papa. "We can't have these little varmint grandkids thinking you made up Scotty's Castle—we've got to go and show them!"

Mimi did not say another word. She just jumped up and ran for the house.

"Woman!" Papa shouted. "Where you goin' in such a goldarn hurry?"

Mimi turned back and gave Papa a big smile. "Why, to pack, of course!"

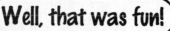

Well, that was fun!

Wow, glad we solved that mystery!

Where shall we go next?

EVERYWHERE!

The End

Now...go to
www.carolemarshmysteries.com
and...

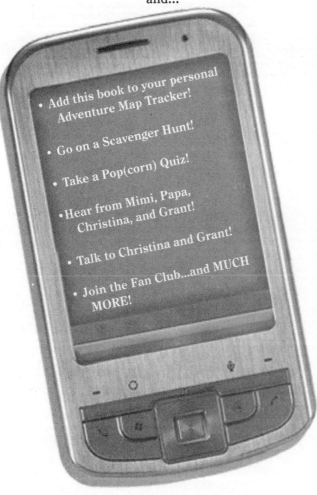

- Add this book to your personal Adventure Map Tracker!

- Go on a Scavenger Hunt!

- Take a Pop(corn) Quiz!

- Hear from Mimi, Papa, Christina, and Grant!

- Talk to Christina and Grant!

- Join the Fan Club...and MUCH MORE!

GLOSSARY

enticing: highly attractive; alluring

infested: having been invaded in great numbers

irrigate: to supply with a constant flow of water

jovial: jolly

kiva: a beehive-shaped fireplace

mirage: an illusion caused by the reflection of light

panorama: an open view in all directions

pirouette: a rapid turn or spin

terracotta: a type of reddish, water-resistant clay

traverse: to travel across or pass over

SAT GLOSSARY

emigrant: someone who leaves one country to settle in another

incredulous: skeptical; unable to believe

instigate: provoke or stir up; incite

itinerary: a plan for travel

ominous: threatening; foretelling evil or something bad

Enjoy this exciting excerpt from:

THE MYSTERY AT Yellowstone National Park

1

BELIEVE IT OR NOT!

Grant began to stir in his rumpled hotel bed sheets, rolling from side to side as he did every morning as he woke up. This morning he had the strange sensation that someone was watching him. He cracked open one eye to see a small lens right in front of his face.

"Christina! What are you doing?" Grant croaked. His sister was standing directly over him with her brand new video camera pointing down at him. Grant whipped the sheet over his head and buried down deep into his feather bed.

"Gooood morning, little brother! It's a marvelous day for a snowmobile ride!" Christina turned her camera toward the window and began filming the snow-covered rolling hills of Cody, Wyoming. "Wow! I can't believe that some people get to look at this view every day. It sure is different than little ol' Peachtree City, Georgia."

Grant slowly crawled out of the covers and sat upright. He rubbed his fingers over his face and through his tousled blond hair. "The only scenery I want to see right now is a loaded breakfast buffet," he said. "I hope they serve real sourdough pancakes out here in the West!"

Christina and Grant had arrived in Cody the night before, along with their grandparents, Mimi and Papa. The kids often traveled with their grandparents while Mimi did research for the children's mystery books she wrote. Mimi always said that the ability to give her grandchildren excitement AND an education was the best job in the world!

Wyoming was one of Papa's favorite parts of the country. One of his fondest memories was a snowmobile tour of Yellowstone National Park that he and Mimi had taken years earlier. A cowboy through and through, Papa was excited to recreate that expedition for his grandchildren. The stop in Cody was a brief layover on the way to what Papa described as a "journey through one of the United States' most valuable treasures." He couldn't wait to put on his cowboy hat and boots and share that treasure with Grant and Christina.

There was a knock at the door adjoining the kids' room to their grandparents' suite.

"Kiddos! You up?" Papa hollered. "We've gotta get a move on—mud pots and geysers and bison await!"

"We're up, Papa!" replied Christina. "We're getting our snow bibs on and packing up our stuff." Christina and Grant loved to snow ski every year with their parents, so luckily they had all the cold weather clothing they would need on this tour. Snowmobiling through the park would be all kinds of fun—but since Yellowstone gets up to 315 inches of snow every year, it would also be all kinds of cold!

Christina stowed her video camera in her backpack. The kids quickly got dressed, gathered their things, and headed to meet Mimi and Papa for breakfast. They were looking forward to filling up with food, and also filling up with the details Papa and Mimi would give them about their trip.

"Papa, when are we getting our snowmobiles?" Grant asked. "I've been practicing my driving skills on my video game. I'm ready to speed all around the trails!" He plopped down at the restaurant table with Frisbee-sized pancakes and greasy bacon spilling off his plate.

Christina's eyes got huge as she put granola and fruit into her yogurt. She had heard there were dangers to look out for throughout the national park, but she never thought it would be her brother on a snowmobile! Luckily, Papa quickly put her mind at ease.

"Oh, I don't think so, cowboy!" Papa said. "You must have a driver's license to operate a snowmobile. The last time I checked, you didn't have one. So, you will be RIDING—not driving on this trip."

As Papa piloted the *Mystery Girl* to Cody the night before, Christina sat in the back of the plane and completed some schoolwork she would miss while she was on the trip, so she hadn't yet asked her grandmother what this winter excursion was all about.

"Ok, Mimi," Christina began, "what's so great about Yellowstone? Why do you and Papa love it so much?"

"Yeah, Mimi," said Grant, "we've been to a national park before. Why is this one any different?"

Mimi pulled her sparkly glasses from her face and smiled at her grandson. "Grant, Yellowstone isn't just *A* national park. It is *THE* national park–the very first national park in the entire world."

"All thanks to President Ulysses S. Grant," said Papa. "He realized that the land and the water and the wildlife here were valuable to the world. So in 1872, he declared that the area would be a national park. As it says on the Roosevelt Arch up at the North Entrance of the park, 'Yellowstone is for the benefit and enjoyment of the people.'"

"So, what are we going to see?" asked Christina, popping a last grape into her mouth. "Oh, Christina," said Mimi, "the park is full of sights and sounds and smells that you could never imagine!"

"That's right," said Papa. "As a matter of fact, when the 19th century explorers began telling the stories about what they saw in this wilderness, people didn't believe them."

"What couldn't they believe?" asked Grant skeptically.

"They couldn't believe what you are getting ready to see on this trip," said Mimi. "Yellowstone National Park is a boiling, bubbling, steaming, gushing, spewing, sizzling, smelly place!"

Grant looked out the window at the sun coming up and glistening off the powder-white snow. "It's freezing cold and there is a ton of snow outside," he said. "I don't see how anything can boil and steam in the dead of winter."

"That's what's so amazing about Yellowstone, young'un," said Papa. "And wait until you see the wildlife—oh, the animals we'll see! Bison, bears, deer, wolves, elk, coyotes, eagles..." his voice trailed off.

Mimi loved to see Papa's eyes light up and the permanent grin attach to his face when he was out in this part of the country.

Christina grabbed her video camera out of her backpack and hit the 'Record' button. "Land that is boiling and steaming? This I gotta see! And film, of course!" she said. "So when do we start?"

"If Grant will wipe that syrup off his chin, we can start right now!" said Papa. "We'll commandeer some snowmobiles and be on our way!"

Grant was excited but also a bit skeptical. As he zipped up his heavy coat and headed to the door with his sister and his grandparents, he secretly hoped that something interesting would crop up during their trip that would add a little thrill to their journey!

He wouldn't have to wait long.

2
REPETITIVE ROUTES

Molly Jane Edwards put rubber bands around her hair braids, stuck her glasses on her face, and let out a sigh. Every year Molly Jane and her parents made the same trip from their house in Jackson Hole, Wyoming to Yellowstone National Park. Her parents were obsessed with the place! For hours, they would watch the mud pots bubble and belch. Or they'd examine and analyze the churning, swirling hot springs and thermal pools or spewing geysers. Her dad could explain how algae could change the color of the water as it tumbled over the Lower Falls, the highest waterfall in the park. Her mom loved the wildflowers and the trees and would **continuously** chirp out their names in English and in Latin!

Without even realizing it, Molly Jane had become something of an expert of the science behind the sights and sounds of Yellowstone. Her parents were great teachers and it was hard not to get swept up in their excitement about these natural wonders, even as they were headed to Flagg Ranch at the park's South Entrance for the sixth time in as many years.

At least this time would be a little different since they were going in the middle of winter. Molly was excited that they would be traveling by snow coach instead of by car. Hopefully there wouldn't be as many traffic jams with snowmobiles and snow coaches as there were with cars during the height of tourist season. Maybe the snow and the trails would shed new light on some of these places in Yellowstone that she knew so well.

If only I had a friend to go with me this time, thought Molly Jane. If only there was a new way to look at the park or a more interesting way to experience its sights. Little did she know there were other kids headed to Yellowstone with the exact same idea!